Harmony Meets the World

"Mother Earth is in you. Not underneath, or above, or around you, but in you. And Father Sun is also in you. You are made of sunshine. You are made of fresh air, or fresh water. To be aware of that wonder, and to value that wonder, can already bring you a lot of happiness."

Thich Nhat Hanh

Book 1
Invitation to the Sun Festival

WRITTEN BY
ERIN K. SCHONAUER & JAMIE C. SCHONAUER

ILLUSTRATIONS BY
KATHLEEN SCHONAUER

INNER PEACE PRESS

Copyright © 2022

All rights reserved. No part of this publication may be reproduced or transmitted, in any form or by any means, without written permission of the publisher except for the use of quotations in a citation.
To request permission, contact the publisher at:
　　　　publisher@innerpeacepress.com
This is a work of fiction. Names, characters, business, events and incidents are the products of the author's imagination. Any resemblance to actual persons, living or dead, or actual events is purely coincidental.

First printing November 2022
Paperback ISBN: 978-1-958150-04-7
Ebook ISBN: 978-1-958150-05-4
Harmony Meets the World: Invitation to the Sun Festival (Book 1)

Subjects:
JUVENILE FICTION / Action & Adventure / General
JUVENILE FICTION / People & Places / General
JUVENILE FICTION / Readers / Chapter Books

Published by **Inner Peace Press**
Eau Claire, Wisconsin, USA
www.innerpeacepress.com

The book series *Harmony Meets the World* was created to bring more connection among all peoples from all cultures, religions, beliefs, and locations.

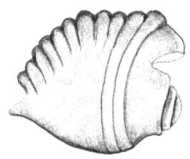

−₹♡₹−

As you read Harmony's story, watch for **glossary words** then check the back of the book for more information on them -- AND add words to your own glossary!

Also, get your scissors out! Cut out your own "Learn the Language" mini-book in Harmony's Journal at the end of the book!

−₹♡₹−

Contents

June Gloom	11
A Hidden Treasure	22
The Sun Temple	30
Sapa Inca	37
The Pututu	49
Plaza de Armas	58
It's Gone!	69
The Secret Tunnel	84
Help!	92
Which Way Out?	108
Ancient Fortress	114
From Shell to Shining Sea	125

Extra Materials

Harmony's Journal	140
Festival Facts	142
Map of Peru	145
Inca Culture	146
Learn the Language	148
Glossary	151
A Taste of Peru	156

Chapter 1
June Gloom

"Ready or not, here I come!" Harmony called. She looked through her binoculars and scanned the beach. The crashing waves softened as they hit the shore. Heavy gray clouds hung in the sky.

Harmony heard a rustling sound behind a big rock near the shore. She tiptoed closer.

"Ah-choo!" someone sneezed.

Harmony looked behind the rock.

"Gotcha!" Harmony exclaimed.

Davis pushed up his glasses and wiggled his nose. "The sea breeze tickles my nostrils," Davis said, scrunching his face as if he just ate a sour lemon.

Davis pointed to a pile of seaweed next to him. It was moving.

"It's Kiwi," Harmony mouthed to Davis. She stepped closer and pulled the seaweed back.

"Hey," Kiwi laughed. He sat in the sand reading his comic book. "You blew my cover."

Harmony looked around the beach. "Where's Meg?" she asked.

Kiwi shrugged his shoulders.

"Aha!" Harmony shouted. She spotted Meg's pink sandals peeking out from behind a pile of **driftwood**. Harmony dashed over.

"Found you!" Harmony exclaimed with excitement.

"No fair. I wasn't ready," Meg said. She twirled out from behind the driftwood. "Twirling is much harder in the sand," she said. She shook her curly hair and continued to spin like a ballerina.

Harmony plopped down in the sand. She looked into the sky with her binoculars.

"Come out, come out, wherever you are," Harmony hollered into the gloomy sky.

"Who are you talking to?" Kiwi asked.

"We're all here," Davis said.

"Yeah, I'm here," Kiwi said. "Davis is here. And Meg's here."

"And you're here," Meg added, pointing to Harmony.

"So, who are you talking to?" Kiwi asked.

"The sun," Harmony said. "You know, the sun – that shining bright star in the sky that makes you feel wonderful inside." Harmony spun around. "I'm so tired of June gloom."

It was June in Harmony's hometown of Crystal Cove, California, and that meant June gloom. The mornings were gloomy with thick gray clouds that didn't budge.

"Even Hermit Crab is crankier than usual," Harmony said. She pointed to the **tide pool** next to her. She watched as her little friend, a **hermit crab**, crawled back into his shell. "He misses the sun, too!" Harmony exclaimed.

"Look," Kiwi said. "The sea star looks like it's shrinking, too." He watched a sea star near them curl up tight.

"EWW," Meg shrieked. "Don't show me those sea creatures. They gross me out."

Harmony was used to Meg squirming over sea critters.

"But you see what I mean," Harmony said. "These little creatures want to see the sun, too."

"You'll never see the sun today," Kiwi said.

"Forget about it, Harmony," Davis said. "You've been looking for the sun all morning."

"It's not happening. You know it's June gloom," Meg said.

"Well, I want the sun!" Harmony exclaimed.

"And I want another round of hide and seek," Kiwi said.

"Me too," Davis agreed.

"You'll never find me this time," Meg called. She ran off.

"Me neither," Kiwi called. He ran down

the shore. His comic book swung at his side.

"I'm prepared to find anything," Harmony said as she covered her eyes. "One, two, three..." She counted slowly to ten. Then she opened her eyes.

"Ready or not, here I come!" Harmony hollered.

She pulled her binoculars up to her eyes and scanned the beach. She saw the lighthouse in the distance. That's where she loved to watch dolphins.

Is Kiwi hiding inside there? Harmony wondered.

She turned in the opposite direction and saw her house. It was a small cottage that sat on a hill overlooking the ocean. *Meg or Davis probably weren't hiding there*, she thought.

Then she saw her school: Abalone Elementary. She knew for certain her friends wouldn't be hiding there. Harmony and her friends just finished second grade and were glad to be on summer break. Harmony was especially happy that she had more time to be an explorer.

Harmony gazed further down the beach. This time, she stopped on an arched rock that sat a few feet off the coastline. It was an unusual rock that looked like an old-fashioned bridge.

Harmony zoomed in with her binoculars on a shiny object that gleamed from underneath the rock. It was a chest – a treasure chest. It had silver and black latches. The sides were worn. It looked like it had been traveling for a long time. Even though it was gloomy and gray outside, the chest glistened.

Harmony ran toward it. Her red boots kicked up the sand as she ran faster and faster. She stopped when she reached the chest.

OMMMMM, a loud, deep sound echoed from inside the chest. Harmony took a step back. The sound stopped.

Harmony took a step closer. Suddenly, the sound started again. *OMMMMM*, the sound vibrated. She felt it in her hands, her heart, even in her toes.

Harmony noticed Hermit Crab crawling toward the treasure chest. He seemed to be following the sound. *OMMMMM.*

"What's inside there?" Harmony asked Hermit Crab.

Chapter 2
A Hidden Treasure

Harmony tiptoed closer to the treasure chest. The loud sound stopped as she opened the lid. She peered inside. A shiny beige shell glistened back.

She lifted the shell out of the chest. It was large. Harmony had to hold it with both hands. It was something she had never

seen before. She'd seen sparkling sea glass, colorful **abalone shells**, and tiny snail shells, but she'd never seen this kind of shell.

"Where did you come from?" Harmony asked the shell.

It was silent.

She looked at Hermit Crab. He was

lying in the sand next to the treasure chest.

"Do you know?" Harmony asked Hermit Crab.

Hermit Crab folded his legs over his tiny black eyes.

"I guess not!" Harmony exclaimed.

Harmony looked closer at the shell. It had a mouthpiece like a trumpet. She pressed her lips to the mouthpiece. She took a deep breath, puffed her cheeks, and blew as hard as she could.

Nothing happened.

Harmony shook the shell.

"Where did the sound go?" Harmony asked Hermit Crab.

He sunk into the sand.

Harmony carefully examined the shell's mouthpiece. She saw a gold paper stuck inside. She pulled it out and unrolled it. A message was written on it. She read it out loud:

"Look south and tune your binoculars to 72 degrees."

Hmmm, Harmony thought. She put the large shell inside her trusty backpack.

Then Harmony glanced at the small compass on top of her binoculars.

Now, look south, Harmony thought.

She turned her body until the needle on her binoculars pointed south.

"Now, 72 degrees," Harmony said. She turned the knobs on her binoculars to 72 degrees. Then she pressed her eyes into her binoculars. Suddenly, an invitation appeared. The words floated in front of her eyepieces.

It read:

"Dear Harmony,

You're invited to **Inti Raymi**, the Sun Festival.

Meet me at the Sun Temple.

Your Friend, Apichu"

As Harmony finished reading the invitation, colors swirled in front of her binoculars. She saw vibrant red and glimmering gold. The colors swirled brighter and brighter.

Suddenly, Harmony felt herself spinning with the colors. She spun faster and faster.

Harmony gripped her binoculars tightly. Her long hair flew in all directions. Her feet lifted off the ground. She spun above the ocean and into the sky. Spinning and spinning. Until...

BOOM BAH! She landed. Her feet hit firm ground.

The strap of her binoculars dug into her neck. Her backpack jostled behind her.

She felt warmth hit her shoulders and face.

"The sun!" Harmony cried. "There it is!" It was like a warm hug.

Harmony looked around in awe. She was standing on top of a hill. It overlooked a beautiful city. There were hilly cobblestone streets, ancient buildings, and people dressed in brightly colored clothing. In the distance, majestic mountains filled the horizon. She wasn't sure where she landed, but she wasn't in her hometown of Crystal Cove anymore. That was for certain.

Chapter 3
The Sun Temple

"Where is this place?" Harmony asked aloud. She was standing next to a large building. It had a massive black-stoned bottom and a cathedral-like top. An arched entrance crowned the front. Harmony wandered inside.

"Beautiful!" Harmony said. Big black stones lined the inside. She brushed her hand against the stones. They were flat and smooth.

Harmony gazed to the far end of the building. She saw a boy waving at her. He looked to be eight-years-old. He ran toward her.

"I see you found the **sun temple**," the boy said. His black hair fell over his eyes. "You must be Harmony." He pushed his hair out of his face.

"Harmony Riley Cruz. That's me!" Harmony smiled.

"I'm Apichu. Apichu Mamani Capac," the boy said. The sun glistened into his dark brown eyes.

"So you're the one who sent me the invitation," Harmony said.

"Yes! Welcome to Peru!" Apichu exclaimed.

"Wowee! Peru!" Harmony beamed.

"Cusco, Peru, to be exact," Apichu said. "My hometown."

"You live here?" Harmony asked.

"Well, not in the Sun Temple," he said. "I live in a house up the road."

"Oh," Harmony laughed.

Harmony examined the temple's stonework walls through her binoculars. She asked, "Who built this temple?"

"My ancestors. The **Inca**," Apichu said.

Harmony let her binoculars dangle around her neck. She touched where two stones met. "The stones are placed together very tightly," Harmony said. She took a strand of her hair and tried to slide it in between two stones. "A piece of hair won't even fit," Harmony said.

"The Inca were known as superior builders for their time," Apichu said. "They didn't even have concrete. They fit the stones together like a puzzle. And it still stands strong today," Apichu explained.

"When did they build this?" Harmony asked.

"Over 800 years ago," Apichu said.

"It's marvelous!" Harmony exclaimed.

Apichu touched the stones. He gazed around the temple. "This is my favorite place to visit. It's where I connect with inti," Apichu said.

"Who's Inti?" Harmony asked.

"The Sun. He's our beloved Inca God," Apichu said.

Harmony looked to the top of the temple. The sun's golden rays split through the open-air window. "Nice to meet you, Inti," Harmony whispered into the stream of light.

"Today is a special day for Inti," Apichu said.

"Why?" Harmony asked.

"Because it's Inti Raymi," Apichu said.

Harmony remembered those words from her invitation.

"What is Inti Raymi?" Harmony asked.

"Inti means sun." Apichu pointed to the sun shining through the temple. "Raymi means festival." Apichu started to dance. "The Sun Festival!" Apichu exclaimed.

"A party for the sun!" Harmony beamed.

"Yes, right here in Cusco. It's one of the biggest festivals in Peru," Apichu said as he danced. "An epic celebration! We do it every year on June 24."

Harmony looked at her watch. "That *is* today!" she exclaimed.

"You're just in time," Apichu said, starting off.

"By the way, why did you invite me?" Harmony asked.

"You were looking for the sun today, weren't you?" Apichu said. "C'mon. The festival is about to start. Let's go!"

Chapter 4
Sapa Inca

Harmony and Apichu entered a terrace overlooking the Sun Temple's courtyard.

"What a view!" Harmony exclaimed.

The green grass shimmered in the early morning sun. Thick stone walls lined the vast open area.

Apichu and Harmony settled into two seats on the terrace.

At once, the sound of flutes began. The soothing melodies carried through the sky. Harmony watched as men, wearing feathered headdresses, entered. They pounded cowhide drums. The THUMP, THUMP, THUMP of the drums thundered through the courtyard. The rhythm was steady and strong.

Soon, dozens of women dressed in red, pink, and gold costumes danced down the temple's steep steps. They moved together gracefully, side by side. Each dancer swayed in line with the rest. When they reached the bottom, they followed each other to the open courtyard. Their black sandals pounded the grassy ground as they danced.

"This is incredible!" Harmony exclaimed.

"It's the first part of the Sun Festival," Apichu said. "After this, the performers will parade through Cusco to two more sacred spots."

Harmony watched more performers enter the courtyard. They sang sweetly and danced in vibrantly colored costumes.

"Most of the performers are from here in Peru. They represent our culture and ancestors," Apichu said. "The Inca tradition is alive today."

Harmony gazed through the lenses of her binoculars. She saw a tall man wearing a gold headdress adorned with feathers. His

red and gold tunic glimmered in the sun.

"Who is that?" Harmony asked.

"The Sapa Inca," Apichu said. "The emperor – the ruler of the land."

"I just can't believe it, an emperor!" Harmony exclaimed.

"He represents an Inca emperor from a long time ago," Apichu said. As the Sapa Inca entered, all of the performers bowed. They knelt to the ground and lowered their heads.

"They bow out of respect," Apichu said.

"Because he's the emperor?" Harmony asked.

"That's right," Apichu nodded.

The Sapa Inca stood boldly on a curved

stone platform facing the rising sun. He outstretched his arms into its beaming light. His palms faced upwards. Soon, he began to speak. His voice was strong and powerful. His words spread out to the sun.

"Who is he speaking to?" Harmony asked.

"Inti," Apichu said. "The Inca sun god."

As the Sapa Inca spoke to the sun, it shone brightly back at him. The Sapa Inca continued to speak boldly. Harmony couldn't understand the language he was speaking. She had never heard it before.

"What language is the Sapa Inca speaking?" Harmony asked Apichu.

"Quechua," Apichu said. "It's an ancient Inca language."

"Quechua," Harmony repeated. "The sun speaks Quechua?" Harmony asked.

"Why, yes," Apichu said. "And so can I. It's my native language. The first language I learned and we speak at home."

Harmony listened to the Sapa Inca speak.

"What is the Sapa Inca saying?" Harmony asked.

Apichu listened for a few seconds. He turned to Harmony. "He's saying: My sun! My father! With great joy we salute you. Basking in your great light. My sun, my father," Apichu explained.

The Sapa Inca bowed.

"We give thanks to the sun for all it provides," Apichu said. "Without the sun our crops couldn't grow."

"And without food from the crops we couldn't survive," Harmony added.

"Like we say: no sun, no life," Apichu said.

"I wonder what it's like to be the sun?" Harmony asked.

"The Inca considered themselves children of the sun," Apichu said.

"Children of the sun?" Harmony wondered out loud.

"Yes, the Inca believed they were descendants of the sun," Apichu said. "They were part of it."

Connected to the sun, Harmony thought. She saw the sun shining on the crowd. It shone on the adults and children. It shone on the lady with an embroidered hat and the boy taking pictures. It shone on everyone in the crowd.

"You know, Apichu. I think we're all connected to the sun," Harmony said.

Apichu smiled. "Me too."

Harmony looked to the temple's curved stone platform. The Sapa Inca finished his speech. As he turned to exit, several men blew into large shells. Their shells had a mouthpiece like a trumpet.

OMMMMM! A loud striking sound bellowed from the shells.

Harmony listened closely. The sound was familiar – very familiar. It was the same sound she heard at home, on the beach. The one that came from the treasure chest.

Harmony pulled her binoculars to her eyes. She zoomed in closer. The men's large shell instruments were just like the one she found on the beach.

Harmony placed her binoculars to her side. She unzipped her backpack and peeked inside at the shell. It was just like the

kind the men were playing.

"Apichu!" Harmony exclaimed. She tapped his shoulder.

Apichu didn't respond. He was captured by the shells' magical sound.

OMMMMM! The deep tone carried through the courtyard.

"Apichu!" Harmony called again.

Apichu's eyes were completely focused on the men who were blowing into the shells.

"Apichu!" Harmony shouted. She tapped his shoulder again.

Suddenly, Apichu snapped out of his daze. He looked at Harmony. "What?" he asked.

"I have a shell like that!" Harmony exclaimed.

Harmony took the shell out of her backpack. She showed it to Apichu.

Apichu looked at the shell. His eyes widened with excitement. "Where did you find this?" he asked.

Chapter 5
The Pututu

"I can't believe it!" Apichu exclaimed. He jumped up and started to dance. "Woo-hoo!" He pumped his fists and wiggled his hips.

Harmony laughed.

"It's my happy dance," Apichu said.

"Why are you dancing?" Harmony asked. She was still holding the shell in her hands.

"You have a **pututu**," Apichu said, smiling.

"A pututu?" Harmony asked.

"You. A pututu," Apichu said as he danced around.

"Who are you calling a pututu?" Harmony asked.

"Not you. The shell in your hand. It's called a pututu," Apichu said.

"A pututu?" Harmony repeated.

"Yes, and it's not just an ordinary pututu. It's a long-lost pututu," Apichu said.

"How do you know that?" Harmony examined the shell.

"Look here," Apichu said, pointing to an

engraving that wrapped around the bottom of the shell. There was an icon of the earth. It was surrounded by rings of circles. The circles made it look like the earth was shaking.

"What does that mean?" Harmony looked at the icon that was engraved on the shell.

"It means this pututu belonged to the Earth Shaker," Apichu said.

"Who's that?" Harmony asked.

"**Pachacutec**. He was known as the Earth Shaker. He was the ninth Sapa Inca and in charge of expanding the Inca Empire. It's said he was the first Sapa Inca to hold the Inti Raymi Festival in the 1400s," Apichu said.

"That's *hundreds* of years ago," Harmony said.

"Yes. Pachacutec must have used this

ancient instrument at the first Inti Raymi Festival," Apichu said.

An ancient instrument, Harmony thought.

"These instruments were an important part of Inti Raymi. The festival was celebrated year after year, for over 100 years," Apichu said.

Harmony listened closely.

"Then it was banned," Apichu said.

"Banned?" Harmony asked.

"Yes, the Spanish invaded and took over the Inca Empire in 1532. Years later, the festival was banned," Apichu said.

"They took the festival away?" Harmony asked.

"Yes, the Spanish stopped the Inca civilization from celebrating Inti Raymi," Apichu said. "Today Inti Raymi is a re-creation of the original Inca festival."

"How do you know all of this?" Harmony asked.

"My grandfather has told me this story many times," Apichu said.

Harmony held the shell in her hands and looked at it with wonder. "So this must be a very special pututu," she said. "That's what you call it, right?"

"Yes. A pututu," Apichu said.

"Pututu." Harmony smiled. "I like that word."

Harmony couldn't believe an emperor from over 600 years ago used this pututu – the very one she held in her hands.

"You know, the whole city of Cusco has been looking for this long-lost pututu," Apichu said.

"And we have it!" Harmony exclaimed.

"Now, it's our job to keep it safe," Apichu said.

"Good idea," Harmony agreed, tucking the pututu into her backpack.

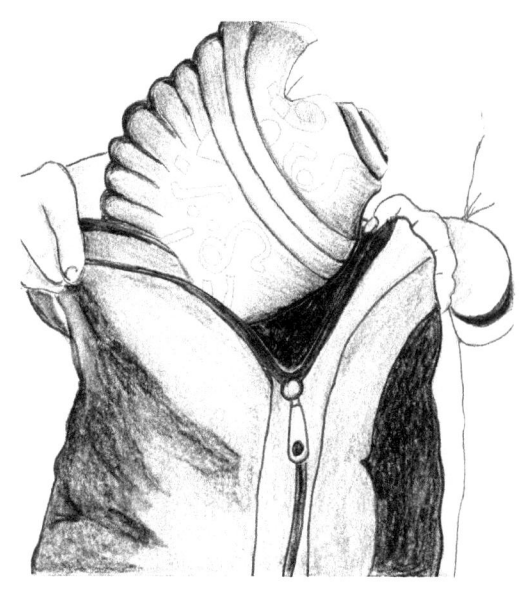

"Let's hurry," Apichu said.

Apichu and Harmony left the Sun Temple's courtyard. They walked out of the Sun Temple and down a hilly cobblestone street that led into the busy city of Cusco.

"Now remember, Harmony, we need to keep the pututu safe," Apichu said.

"It's safe in my backpack," Harmony said.

Apichu thought for a moment. "We must return the pututu to the Sapa Inca," he said.

"You mean the emperor we saw at the Sun Temple this morning?" Harmony asked.

"Yes, he'll know what to do with it," Apichu said. "But we need to return it quickly. Before the festival ends."

"How are we going to find the Sapa Inca?" Harmony asked. She watched the crowd grow bigger.

"I know," Apichu called.

"You do?" Harmony asked.

"Trust me," Apichu said as he ran off. "Catch me if you can!" he called to Harmony. Harmony watched as Apichu was swallowed into the huge crowd.

Chapter 6
Plaza de Armas

Harmony dashed through the crowd of people. She wanted to find Apichu, but she couldn't see him anywhere.

"Apichu," she called. Her voice traveled into the crowd.

"Ap-pi-chuuuuuu," she called again.

He was nowhere to be found.

Harmony saw people gathering at a

plaza nearby. It was about a block away. Harmony squeezed through the crowd until she reached the plaza. It was a large town square with cobblestone streets. It felt ancient and magical. There were colorful flags fluttering in the wind. In the middle of the plaza there was a bronze statue of a man. He looked like an important emperor. Harmony walked to the statue. She saw the name Pachacutec engraved on the front.

"So, you're the emperor Apichu was talking about," Harmony said to the statue. "You're the Earth Shaker. We have your pututu. We will return it to the Sapa Inca. But first I need to find Apichu."

Harmony searched for Apichu. To her left, she saw a tall church. To her right, she saw more crowds of people.

"Where did he go?" Harmony asked. She pulled up her binoculars and scanned the crowd. Suddenly, she stopped.

"Aha!" Harmony exclaimed. She spotted Apichu's bright **poncho** among the crowd. "Apichu," Harmony called as she ran up to him.

"I see you found me," he laughed.

"Very funny," Harmony said out of breath.

"Welcome to **plaza de Armas**," Apichu said.

"It's beautiful," Harmony said, still trying to catch her breath.

"Plaza de Armas is the center of Cusco. It was the heart of the Inca Empire," Apichu said.

Harmony watched as the parade of performers entered the plaza. There were so many different colors and people moving.

"This is where the second part of Inti Raymi takes place," Apichu said. "The Sapa Inca will be here soon."

"Then we can give him the pututu," Harmony said.

"He's going to be so proud of us!" Apichu exclaimed.

Harmony watched as dozens of men, dressed in long blue shirts, called tunics, ran in unison. They moved together, each holding a rectangle shield designed with bright geometric shapes.

"They are Inca warriors," Apichu said.

"Incredible," Harmony said. "I've never seen anything like this before."

Moments later, men, dressed in red, entered the plaza. Each man swept the ground with a branch. *SWISH. SWISH. SWISH.* The branches swayed from side to side, whisking the ground.

"What are they doing?" Harmony asked Apichu.

"They're sweeping away the evil spirits," Apichu said.

"Evil spirits?" Harmony asked, slightly alarmed, as she watched the men sweep.

"Well, just in case there are any evil spirits. They must be removed before the Sapa Inca arrives," Apichu said.

More performers paraded by. The hot sun beat down on Harmony's face. "Whew, the sun is hot," she said. "My binoculars are even sweating." Apichu laughed at her.

Soon, women entered the plaza. They walked gracefully as they tossed yellow flower petals into the air. The petals floated up into the sky then landed softly on the ground.

"It looks like a golden carpet," Harmony said.

"The yellow flowers signal the queen is coming," Apichu said.

"There she is," Harmony exclaimed as she pointed ahead.

The queen entered.

"She's called the **coya**," Apichu said.

Harmony watched as an elegant woman, dressed in a white and red dress, sat in a chair atop a large rectangular platform. She was carried by twenty men who were all dressed in green.

"She's so beautiful!" Harmony said. "And graceful," she added.

The sun glistened off the queen's silver headdress. Her black braids hung perfectly over her shoulders. She held a big bouquet of flowers on her lap.

Apichu turned to Harmony. "Now that the queen is here, the Sapa Inca will come next."

Apichu's eyes beamed with excitement. "Then we can give him the pututu."

Harmony and Apichu turned their heads. At once, the Sapa Inca entered. His presence was strong and powerful. He stood on a large platform carried by several men. The Sapa Inca waved to the crowd. Apichu waved to him. Then Harmony did too.

"Hurry," Apichu said to Harmony. "Get out the pututu."

The Sapa Inca came closer to them.

Harmony took off her backpack.

"He's almost here," Apichu said. "Hurry!"

Harmony unzipped her backpack.

"Quick, Harmony. Get out the pututu," Apichu urged.

Harmony opened her backpack.

Apichu waited anxiously.

Harmony looked inside her backpack.

"It's gone," she gasped.

Chapter 7
It's Gone!

"Gone? What do you mean it's gone?" Apichu asked.

"The pututu. It's gone," Harmony said.

"I thought you put it inside your backpack," Apichu said.

"I did," Harmony said. She rifled through her backpack.

"So, where is it?" Apichu asked.

"I don't know," Harmony said. She showed Apichu her empty backpack.

"That's impossible!" Apichu exclaimed.

"How will we find it?" Harmony asked.

Apichu looked around their feet. "It's not here," he said.

Apichu and Harmony scanned the plaza. It was packed with spectators and festival performers.

"It can't be there," Apichu said as he pointed to a fancy church with two bell towers. "We didn't even go there."

"That's true," Harmony said.

"And we didn't walk over there." Apichu pointed to the statue of Pachacutec.

"I did!" Harmony exclaimed. "Follow me."

Harmony and Apichu squeezed their way through the crowd.

Soon, they arrived at the bronze statue of the emperor Pachacutec. They searched for the pututu.

"It's not here," Harmony said.

"Now what?" Apichu asked, frantically searching the area.

Harmony paused and thought for a moment. "Maybe I left the pututu at the Sun Temple," she said.

"Good thought. But we have to find it fast! Before the festival ends!" Apichu exclaimed. "I know a shortcut. Follow me."

Harmony followed Apichu out of the crowd.

Moments later, they came to a side street. Apichu stopped at a sign that read: *San Pedro Market*.

"Through here," he said.

Apichu and Harmony entered the market.

"I'm so thirsty," Apichu said.

"Me too," Harmony agreed.

"I know the perfect place to get something to drink," Apichu said.

As Harmony and Apichu walked through the market, there were loads of fresh fruits, vegetables, and spices all around.

"It smells wonderful in here," Harmony smiled.

"It's the **huacatay** you smell. It is a Peruvian mint," Apichu said, pointing to colorful baskets filled with green, leafy herbs.

Harmony took in the refreshing scent. It smelled like mint, licorice, and citrus.

"The drink stand is up here," Apichu said, pointing ahead. "Plus, I want you to meet someone."

"Who do you want me to meet?" Harmony asked.

She spotted an older woman strolling through the market with a llama. "I know,"

Harmony said. "You want me to meet your pet llama!" she exclaimed.

"Nope," Apichu laughed.

"Who then?" Harmony asked.

"You'll see," Apichu said.

Harmony saw a vegetable stand lined with sacks of potatoes.

"You want me to meet your favorite vegetable?" Harmony guessed, pointing to the potatoes.

"Double nope," Apichu said.

Harmony saw a group of kids eating at a table nearby.

"Your friends?" Harmony asked.

"Closer," Apichu said.

Soon, they stopped at a small drink stand. The woman standing behind it smiled at them.

"My **mantay**!" Apichu exclaimed.

"Mantay?" Harmony asked.

"My mother!" Apichu said. "Mantay is Quechua for mother!"

Apichu pointed to the woman standing behind the drink stand. She waved. Apichu gave her a hug.

"Hello. Or as we say in our Quechua language, *Allillanchu*," Apichu's mother said as she turned to Harmony. "I'm Mrs. Capac."

"Nice to meet you," Harmony greeted her with a smile. "I'm Harmony."

Apichu's mother poured a purple drink into a tall glass. "Would you like some?" she asked Harmony.

Harmony looked at the liquid in the glass. "It's purple!" she said.

"It's *chicha morada*," Apichu explained.

"It's made from purple corn," Mrs. Capac said. "Try it." She handed Harmony the glass.

Harmony took a sip. "Mmmm, so delicious," she said.

"It's a popular Peruvian drink," Apichu said.

Apichu's mother poured Apichu a glass. He took a big gulp.

"It's my favorite drink," Apichu said.

Harmony took another sip. "You know, this reminds me of a special drink my grandmother makes. It's made from a purple berry called açai. Her drink is purple, too!"

"It's purple like this?" Apichu asked, holding up the glass.

"Yes," Harmony said. "My grandma and I drink açai smoothies together on hot summer days at the beach. She always makes jokes while we drink it. We smile and sip together." Harmony smiled. *I love my grandma*, thought Harmony. She sipped her chicha morada. "A taste of home!" Harmony exclaimed.

"And a taste of Peru!" Apichu said. He raised his glass in cheers to Harmony. The purple drink swirled in his glass. "We grow this special purple corn locally. It's dried for many days in the Peruvian sunshine," Apichu said.

Harmony and Apichu both took another sip.

"Wow, I can taste the sunshine in my drink," Harmony said after she swallowed.

"Without the sun we wouldn't have purple corn," Apichu said.

"Or this amazing drink!" Harmony exclaimed. "Sunshine and goodness down to the last sip," Harmony said as she finished her drink.

"Thanks, Mantay," Apichu said as he gulped down the rest of his drink.

"Thank you, Mrs. Capac," Harmony said, returning her glass.

"You're welcome!" Mrs. Capac said.

"I'll see you at dinner," Apichu called.

"Enjoy the festival," Mrs. Capac said, smiling as she waved.

Apichu and Harmony walked out of the

market and onto a narrow cobblestone side street.

"C'mon, Harmony, time is running short. We have to find the pututu before the festival ends. The performers will soon arrive at their final destination, the ancient fortress of **Sacsayhuaman**," Apichu said.

Harmony picked up her pace. "Wowee. The chicha morada gave me tons of energy," Harmony said. "Makes me feel like doing the crab walk."

"Crab walk?" Apichu asked.

"Yeah, crabs are my favorite critters on the beach. It's fun to walk like them," Harmony said. She crouched to the ground and stuck her belly up. She used her arms and legs to walk like a crab. "Try it," she said.

Apichu tried.

"This is what I do with my friends," Harmony said.

Apichu couldn't coordinate his arms with his legs. "I feel like a broken crab," he said.

"Keep going. You'll get it," Harmony called. Her legs and arms fluttered across the ground.

Apichu's legs gave out. "Forget it," Apichu said.

He stood up. "I'll do the Sapa Inca walk," Apichu said. He straightened his posture, jutted his chin forward, and swung his arms at his sides.

"You do look like the Sapa Inca," Harmony said. She was still doing the crab walk.

Apichu walked boldly pretending he was the Sapa Inca. "We can do this, Harmony! We can find the pututu."

"Yes, we can. We have a mission ahead," Harmony said.

Apichu and Harmony continued down the cobblestone street – on their mission to find the pututu.

Chapter 8
The Secret Tunnel

Harmony and Apichu arrived at the Sun Temple's courtyard.

"Look," Harmony pointed to the temple's curved black stone wall. "There it is," she said in wonder as she pulled her binoculars from her face.

The pututu sat on top of the wall.

"C'mon," Apichu said. "Let's get it."

Harmony and Apichu raced toward the pututu.

Suddenly, the loud sound of drums thundered in the distance.

"What's that?" Harmony asked.

"The drums from the festival. The performers are traveling toward their final destination, the ancient fortress," Apichu said.

THUMP. THUMP. THUMP. The drums thundered again.

"Oh, no!" Harmony exclaimed.

"What's the matter?" Apichu asked.

"Look!" Harmony pointed ahead. The pututu teetered back and forth on the wall's edge. With each THUMP, the pututu teetered more. It barely sat on top.

"It's going to fall," Apichu said.

"It can't fall!" Harmony cried.

The pututu teetered even more.

Harmony and Apichu ran closer.

"Too late," Harmony said. She watched the pututu fall off the temple's curved wall.

Harmony put her binoculars to her eyes and looked over the edge. She saw the pututu roll down the hill below.

"We have to get it!" Apichu called. He started running after it.

"I'm right behind you," Harmony said, following closely.

Apichu and Harmony ran out of the courtyard, through the Sun Temple, and down the hill. Apichu looked in the distance and saw the pututu lying in the street.

"There it is!" Apichu charged toward it.

"Wait!" Harmony warned. She saw a truck, carrying loads of fruit, drive straight toward the pututu. "The truck's going to hit it!"

Apichu ran faster.

"I'll save it!" Apichu said. He dove for the pututu.

The fruit truck turned quickly down a side street, swerving around the pututu.

Apichu slid on his knees, trying to grab

the pututu. It slipped through his hands and rolled away.

"Oh, no! The pututu," he cried. His hands slid along the cobblestone street.

Suddenly, the street started to move apart. A huge opening appeared and the pututu fell inside.

"Are you okay?" Harmony asked, catching up to Apichu.

"Yes, but the pututu fell down there," Apichu said, pointing to the gap in the street. Apichu and Harmony examined the cobblestone street. A vast, dark hole stared back at them.

"Woah!" They both exclaimed.

"This must be it," Apichu said.

"What?" Harmony asked.

"The **chinkanas**," Apichu said. "The tunnels."

"There are tunnels under the city?" Harmony asked, looking into the wide opening.

"Yes. They are secret tunnels. It's said they were made by the ancient Inca. The tunnels are hidden around the city," Apichu told Harmony.

"Looks like we just found one," Harmony said.

"Let's go in!" Apichu exclaimed.

"You want to go in *there*?" Harmony asked, looking into the dark tunnel.

Apichu shook his head. "For the sake of the pututu," he said, trying to convince Harmony.

Harmony gazed into the tunnel. It looked dark and cold.

"I don't know," she said. She took a step back.

"C'mon," Apichu called. He climbed into the tunnel and disappeared into the darkness.

Chapter 9
Help!

"Help!" Apichu called from inside the tunnel. Harmony looked inside.

"My foot. It's caught!" Apichu exclaimed.

"Hold still. I'm coming," Harmony called. She slid into the narrow underground tunnel. It was pitch black.

"Hurry," Apichu called. "I can't move my foot. It's stuck."

"On what?" Harmony asked.

"I don't know. It feels slippery and tight," Apichu said.

Harmony moved closer to Apichu. She searched for his foot in the darkness. She felt something slippery and tight around Apichu's foot.

"It feels like a -- ," Harmony began.

"Snake!" They both yelled.

Harmony jumped back. Apichu shook his foot. Harmony flicked her binoculars to night vision mode. She looked closer.

"False alarm!" Harmony exclaimed. "It's a rope. Covered in moss." She examined it through her binoculars. Then she looked above her. She saw the mossy rope hanging above. "Looks like the rope dropped from the ceiling when you entered," Harmony explained. "And then hooked your foot."

"A booby trap," Apichu said. "Legend has it the *chinkanas* are filled with booby traps."

"We should definitely *not* be down here," Harmony said.

"But we need to find the pututu," Apichu insisted.

Harmony untied the rope from Apichu's foot.

"Thanks," Apichu said as he stood up.

Harmony looked further down the tunnel with her binoculars set to night vision.

"Oh, no," Harmony exclaimed.

"What?" Apichu asked.

"We have to turn around," Harmony said.

"No way. We must find the pututu. It fell down here somewhere," Apichu explained.

"It's too dangerous," Harmony said. "I can see that there are more obstacles ahead." She peered through her binoculars toward the path in front of them. "Look," Harmony said as she handed Apichu her binoculars.

He looked through them. He saw huge boulders, wide-open holes, and twisting pathways.

"You're right. Let's turn around," Apichu trembled.

Apichu and Harmony turned to leave.

THUD! A large, heavy stone wall dropped in front of them, nearly missing their toes.

"Whoa!" They shrieked.

"Guess there's no turning back," Harmony said.

"What are we going to do?" Apichu asked.

"We must keep going," Harmony said. She peered through her binoculars and led the way. The darkness surrounded them. "It's so scary and dark in here," Harmony quivered. "This is how dark it would be without the sun."

"Nothing could exist without the sun," Apichu said.

Harmony shivered as a cold draft skimmed her shoulders. It was completely silent. "We're all alone," she whispered.

"**Pachamama** is here," Apichu said.

"Who?" Harmony asked.

"Pachamama. That means Mother Earth in Quechua," Apichu said. He touched the dirt walls.

Harmony examined the tunnel walls through her binoculars. They were made of dirt. Mother Earth's dirt. And so was the ground they walked on. Mother Earth was beneath them, above them, and on both sides of them. They were inside Mother Earth.

"The Inca respect and praise Pachamama. She is a special goddess," Apichu said.

"Maybe Pachamama will help us," Harmony said.

She looked through her binoculars. "Uh, oh!" Harmony exclaimed. A huge boulder sat in front of them. "We need to cross this boulder." She ran her hand across its rough surface. It was as big as a haystack. "It looks unsteady," Harmony called to Apichu. "And there's a muddy pit between this boulder and the path ahead."

"How will we cross it?" Harmony asked as she handed Apichu the binoculars. He peered through them.

"We have to trust Pachamama," Apichu said.

Harmony thought for a moment. "Since we are inside Mother Earth, let's think and act like Mother Earth."

"We are powerful like Mother Earth," Apichu said.

"And strong like her boulders," Harmony said. She pressed her hands on top of the boulder and pushed herself up. She crouched on top. "It's rocking," she said.

"Keep your balance," Apichu said.

"I'm trying. I don't want to fall into the muddy pit," Harmony called. Her toes gripped the rock's edge.

"Keep calm," Apichu said. "I have an idea."

Apichu put his foot onto the boulder.

"The boulder is still moving," Harmony called. Her foot slipped.

"Pull your foot in and stand up," Apichu said.

"I can't," Harmony called.

"Be powerful like Pachamama," Apichu reminded Harmony.

Harmony took a deep breath. She pulled her foot toward her body and slowly stood up. Apichu put his hands on top of the boulder.

"The boulder is tipping again," Harmony said.

"Stand still. I'm coming," Apichu said.

Apichu pushed himself onto the other side of the boulder. He crouched into a ball. Suddenly, Harmony and Apichu balanced on the boulder like they were on a teeter totter.

"We're balancing!" Harmony exclaimed.

"Balance. Like Pachamama. She has balance. Fire and water," Apichu said.

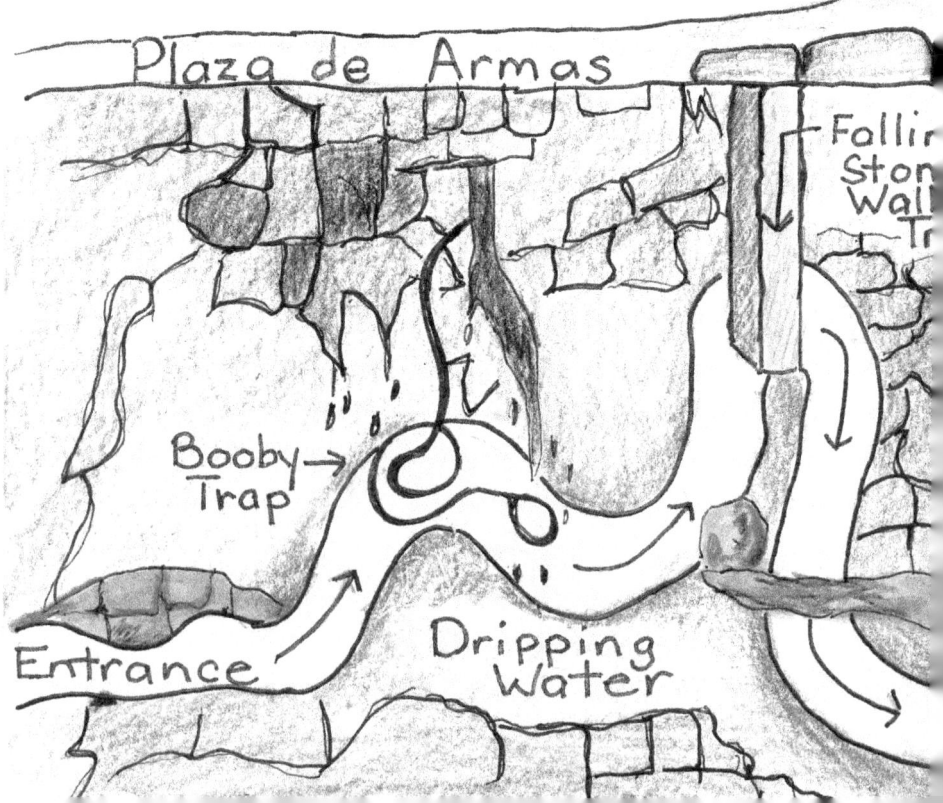

"And we do, too," Harmony said. She looked ahead with her binoculars. "I see it! The pututu! It's on the other side of the muddy pit."

"We have to jump over the pit and onto the path," Apichu said.

"Over the pit?" Harmony asked, her voice quivering.

"And onto the path," Apichu repeated in a reassuring voice.

"You go first," Harmony said.

"We have to jump together," Apichu said. "Otherwise, the boulder will tip."

"But we have to jump big," Harmony said. "We can't fall down there." She pointed to the deep pit below.

"There might be more booby traps," Apichu said, looking down into the vast pit. It looked endless and terrifying.

"Ready?" Apichu asked Harmony.

"Ready as I'll ever be," Harmony sighed.

Harmony and Apichu took a deep breath.

"On the count of three," Apichu said.

Harmony bent her knees ready to jump.

"One, two, three," Apichu called.

Harmony and Apichu both jumped. They flew over the muddy pit and onto the dirt path on the other side. They tumbled to the ground. Dirt flew in all directions.

"We did it!" Harmony exclaimed, brushing the dirt off her hands.

"I knew we could!" Apichu agreed, dusting the dirt off his clothes.

"Now, we can get the pututu," Harmony said.

Harmony and Apichu looked down the path.

"Where's the pututu?" Harmony asked.

"I don't know," Apichu said.

They walked further down the path. Harmony led the way as she peered through her night vision binoculars.

"Uh, oh!" Harmony exclaimed.

"What?" Apichu asked.

"Looks like the path splits into two different directions," Harmony said.

"Let's see," Apichu said.

Harmony handed Apichu the night vision binoculars. He looked through them.

"Oh, no!" Apichu called.

"Which way should we take?" They both asked at the same time.

Chapter 10
Which Way Out?

𝓗armony and Apichu stood in front of the divided path.

"Let's go left," Harmony said as she looked at the illuminated compass on top of her binoculars.

"I think we should go right," Apichu said.

"The path to the left leads east," Harmony said. "I think we should go east."

"Why?" Apichu asked.

"The sun rose in the east this morning. That's when we were at the Sun Temple," Harmony said.

"Yes, that's when the Sapa Inca gave his powerful speech to the sun god, Inti," Apichu said.

"Hopefully, this path will lead back to the Sun Temple," Harmony said as she started down the path.

"If there are more booby traps down here, it's your fault," Apichu said, joking. He followed Harmony down the dark path.

"The coast is clear," Harmony said as she looked through her night vision binoculars.

"So far," Apichu said unsteadily.

Suddenly, drums thundered above them. They could feel the vibrations in their feet.

"You hear that?" Harmony asked.

"It's the sound of cow-hide drums from the festival," Apichu's voice started to perk up with a sense of hope.

"Let's follow the sound," Harmony said.

"Yes, the performers are probably moving toward the ancient fortress of Sacsayhuaman," Apichu said, following close to Harmony. "The ancient fortress is the final part of the Sun Festival."

"Now, I can hear drums and flutes," Harmony said.

"Me too," Apichu said. "Keep following the sound."

The melody of the flutes and drums got louder. Soon, they heard feet pounding against the ground.

Harmony led the way, keeping pace with the sounds.

"Keep going, Harmony. You're doing great," Apichu encouraged.

Harmony and Apichu walked faster. They heard sounds coming from the instruments and performers. They could feel the vibrations within the ground.

The darkness swallowed them as they continued along.

Harmony looked further down the tunnel. "Look!" she exclaimed.

"What?" Apichu looked ahead. And then he saw it.

"Sunlight!" Harmony cried. A golden stream of light glistened at the end of the pitch-black tunnel.

"Hurry," Apichu said. "It's our way out."

Harmony and Apichu charged toward the small stream of light. The glowing sunlight shone on a sparkling object. Harmony zoomed in on it.

"You'll never believe it!" Harmony beamed.

"What?" Apichu asked.

"The pututu!" Harmony exclaimed.

"Are you serious?" Apichu asked, trying to get a look.

"Yes, I'm absolutely serious," Harmony said.

Apichu looked ahead and saw the pututu shining in the sunlight. "It *is* the pututu," he said. As Harmony and Apichu came within a few feet of it, the pututu started to move.

"It's moving," Harmony said in amazement.

"It *is* moving," Apichu gasped.

Harmony and Apichu chased the pututu. The pututu slipped through a crack at the end of the tunnel.

Chapter 11
Ancient Fortress

"The pututu moved through there," Harmony pointed to the small crack in the tunnel.

"Let's push this stone here," Apichu said, pointing to a large stone above the crack.

"On the count of three," Harmony said.

"One, two, three," they counted.

They pushed the large stone with all their might.

Along with the large stone, the two new friends tumbled out of the dark tunnel and onto a steep hill. The bright sunlight hit their faces.

"We did it!" Harmony exclaimed.

"Yes, we did!" Apichu cried.

"The sun guided us out of the tunnel," Harmony said in relief.

"Thank you, Inti!" Apichu shouted.

Apichu and Harmony gazed around. They were sitting on top of a hill that overlooked the ancient fortress, Sacsayhuaman.

"Look," Apichu said, pointing to the pututu. It was moving quickly through the grassy hilltop.

Harmony and Apichu stood up and raced toward it.

"How is it moving?" Harmony asked. She zoomed in on her binoculars.

"It has legs!" Harmony gasped.

She saw little red legs moving from underneath the pututu. Harmony picked it up. She looked inside the shell.

"Hermit Crab!" she exclaimed. "You were inside the shell the whole time?"

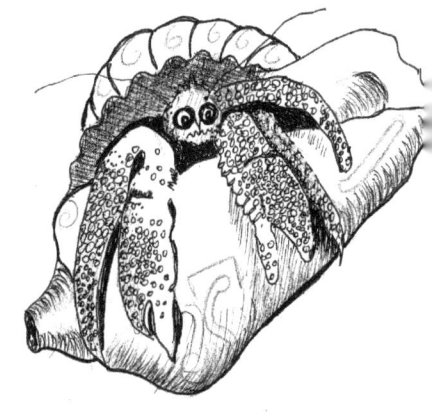

"How did that critter get in there?" Apichu asked.

"Hermit Crab must have snuck into my backpack when I was at home on the beach," Harmony said.

"Now, *that's* a crab walk," Apichu said.

Harmony laughed. She took Hermit Crab out of the pututu. "Oh, Hermit Crab. You're such a jokester," Harmony said. She placed Hermit Crab into her backpack.

"You hold this," Harmony said, handing the pututu to Apichu.

"The Sapa Inca will arrive soon," Apichu said. "Then we can give it to him."

Soon, sounds of drums and flutes filled the ancient fortress. Harmony and Apichu watched as hundreds of dancers entered.

"The final part of Inti Raymi is starting," Apichu said.

Men wearing tall red and orange headdresses entered the arena in groups.

"Who are they?" Harmony asked.

"Those men represent the people from the Amazon," Apichu told Harmony.

Harmony grabbed her binoculars.

"Each group of performers that enters represent the four **suyus** – the four regions or areas of land of the Inca Empire," Apichu said.

Apichu and Harmony watched as people from the Amazon and the Highlands entered the large outdoor area.

"This is exciting," Harmony said.

Apichu held the pututu firmly. As Harmony and Apichu looked across the grassy field, they saw the Sapa Inca enter.

"There he is!" Apichu exclaimed.

"And this time we have the pututu in our hands," Harmony said.

The Sapa Inca turned and started to veer away.

"How will we get him to see us?" Harmony asked.

"I know what to do!" Apichu said. He raised the pututu to his mouth and blew into it.

OMMMMM. A loud, deep sound vibrated throughout the fortress.

At once, the Sapa Inca turned around. He stared at Apichu and Harmony. He walked toward them. His steps were bold and his gold headdress shone brilliantly in the sun. The Sapa Inca stopped in front of Apichu and Harmony.

"Bow," Apichu whispered to Harmony.

Harmony and Apichu knelt to the ground and bowed their heads in his presence. After a few moments, they stood.

"We have Pachacutec's pututu," Apichu said softly. He handed it to the Sapa Inca.

The Sapa Inca caressed the pututu

in his hands as if it was a precious jewel. "Thank you, my children. My children of the sun," he said.

Apichu and Harmony smiled. A ray of sunlight shone over them. The Sapa Inca raised his hands to the sun then placed each one on Apichu and Harmony's shoulders.

"Just remember," the Sapa Inca said. "Father Sun is in all of us."

Harmony felt warmth in her heart. She liked that she was connected to the sun. She looked around the large outdoor fortress. There were thousands and thousands of spectators and performers. The sun was shining on all of them – every one of them.

The sun is in everyone. We are all connected, Harmony thought.

The Sapa Inca nodded in gratitude and turned away.

Apichu and Harmony bowed deeply.

The Sapa Inca walked boldly up a staircase and onto a stone platform. The thousands of spectators and performers became silent.

"He's going to recite his final speech," Apichu whispered to Harmony.

The Sapa Inca stood on top of the stone platform. He outstretched his arms to the sun. His bold voice started in the Quechua language. Apichu translated for Harmony:

"Father of us all, draw us to your side. Listen to us. Bless us. Drive us down the correct life path. Powerful god, you are the one who carries the life of men in this new beginning and at the end. Never forget us; we are in your hands. Grant us always a pleasant and soft existence." The Sapa Inca stood tall. His presence was powerful.

Then, the Sapa Inca took the pututu that Apichu and Harmony gave him and blew into it. *OMMMMM*. The loud sound traveled through the ancient fortress of Sacsayhuaman.

Harmony felt the sound vibrate through her body. Apichu felt it, too.

The Sapa Inca walked down the steps. As he turned to exit, he nodded to Apichu and Harmony. The performers followed the Sapa Inca and trailed out of the ancient fortress. In the distance, the sun was setting, casting shadows throughout the grassy field and hilltops.

"Wow," Harmony said to Apichu. "That was spectacular."

Suddenly, Hermit Crab stuck his head out of Harmony's backpack. Harmony took him out and held him in her hands.

"We need to go home," Harmony told Hermit Crab. "But how?"

Chapter 12
From Shell to Shining Sea

Harmony and Apichu watched as the sun lowered over the horizon.

"I have to get home," Harmony told Apichu.

"Already?" Apichu asked.

"I need to return Hermit Crab to the beach," Harmony said. "And see my friends and family back home."

She looked at Hermit Crab. "Do you know how to get home?" she asked. He covered his eyes.

"How did you get here this morning?" Apichu asked Harmony.

She unzipped her backpack and took out the piece of paper she had saved. "From this secret code," she said, showing Apichu the paper. "I found it inside the pututu. It was in the treasure chest on the beach. It said to point my binoculars south and tune them to 72 degrees." She thought for a moment. "Maybe I should reverse the code. That means I need to point my binoculars north to go home," Harmony said.

"Makes sense," Apichu agreed.

Harmony grasped her binoculars.

"I wish we had more time," Apichu said.

"Me, too," Harmony agreed.

"Do you have a switch on your binoculars to make the day longer?" Apichu asked.

"I wish," Harmony laughed.

"We do make a good team," Apichu said.

"And you really taught me a lot," Harmony smiled. "I'll never forget what a pututu is!"

"And I'll never forget your crabwalk," Apichu laughed.

Harmony lifted her binoculars. "Well, I guess it's time. Time to go." She turned until the needle on her binoculars pointed north. She pressed her eyes into her binoculars. She saw the sun cast a shadow over the mountains. It was a sun shadow. Harmony zoomed in. The shadow read: 118 degrees.

"118 degrees. That's my way home!" she called.

"Hey, Harmony. Look at this," Apichu called. He was doing the crabwalk.

"You're doing it!" Harmony smiled.

Hermit Crab clapped.

"I'll miss you," Apichu called. He was still doing the crab walk.

"I'll miss you, too, Apichu," Harmony called.

Harmony turned the knobs on her binoculars to 118 degrees. She felt herself starting to spin.

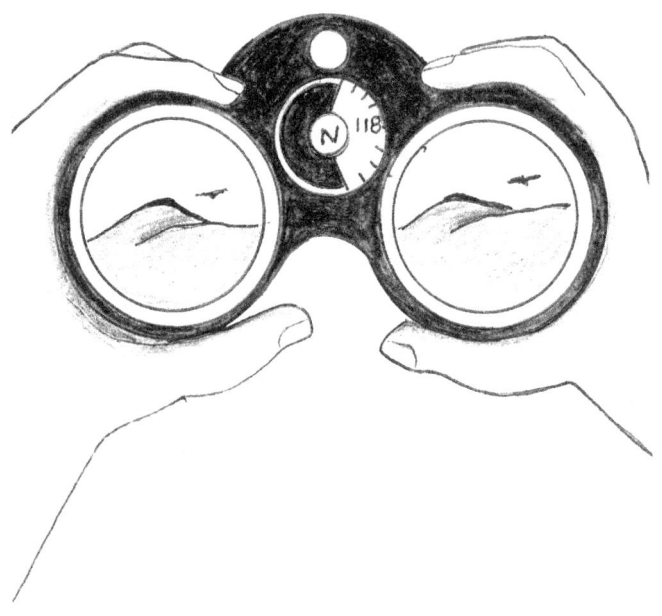

"Bye, Apichu," Harmony called as she swirled. "Visit me anytime!"

Apichu waved. "*Tupananchiscama,*" he called. "See you next time." He watched as Harmony swirled into the setting sun. She spun faster and faster.

Spinning and spinning. Until...

BOOM BAH! She landed. Her feet hit firm ground.

Harmony opened her eyes. She was standing on the beach. She was back home in Crystal Cove. The treasure chest was still open. The waves were still crashing against the shore. And her friends were still hiding for their game of hide and seek.

"Wowee!" Harmony exclaimed. "A time warp." It was still morning. No time had passed. Harmony was standing in the same spot that she was in before her great adventure. She still had her binoculars around her neck. Her backpack was still strapped to her shoulders. And Hermit Crab was caressed in her hands.

Harmony carefully placed Hermit Crab back into the tide pool. He splashed in the shallow water. A little smile streamed across his face.

"Did I see a smile?" Harmony asked Hermit Crab.

Hermit Crab spun in a circle. Then, he pointed his leg at the treasure chest.

All of a sudden, the chest moved into the side of the rock. It took on the rock's shape and color.

"Whoa! Did you do that, Hermit Crab?" Harmony asked.

Hermit Crab folded his little legs over his tiny black eyes.

Harmony examined the rock. The treasure chest's black latches were barely visible. The chest was camouflaged and safely hidden in the rock.

"Let this be our little secret," Harmony told Hermit Crab. He shook his head and splashed in the tide pool.

Harmony strolled down the beach.

After a few steps, she stopped and looked back at the treasure chest. *I wonder if I'll see the treasure chest again?* she thought. *And if I do, what will be inside it next time?*

Harmony dashed down the beach looking for her friends. She had almost forgotten about their game of hide and seek. She couldn't wait to see them.

"Come out, come out, wherever you are!" Harmony called to them. She saw Kiwi run out from behind the bushes.

"I knew you wouldn't find me," Kiwi said as he ran toward Harmony.

"Stumped ya!" Davis called as he climbed out from behind a rock.

"I'm not sharing my secret hiding spot," Meg said. She twirled down the beach toward Harmony.

"You got me," Harmony said, smiling.

Suddenly, a gust of wind whipped through the air. A big, gray cloud darkened the sky.

"Guess the sun never came out this morning," Kiwi said.

"Oh well," Davis muttered.

"Maybe tomorrow," Meg said.

"The clouds might be blocking the sun, but we know it is up there – keeping us connected," Harmony shared.

"Harmony!" a voice called from a distance.

"My grandma's calling me," Harmony said. "Got to go!"

"See you tomorrow," Kiwi shouted.

"Later, Harmony," Davis called.

"Bye," Meg said as she twirled down the beach.

"Goodbye," Harmony waved. She walked toward her house. Then she stopped and looked into the gray, gloomy sky.

"Thanks for everything, Inti. My life-giving sun," Harmony said, smiling to the cloudy sky.

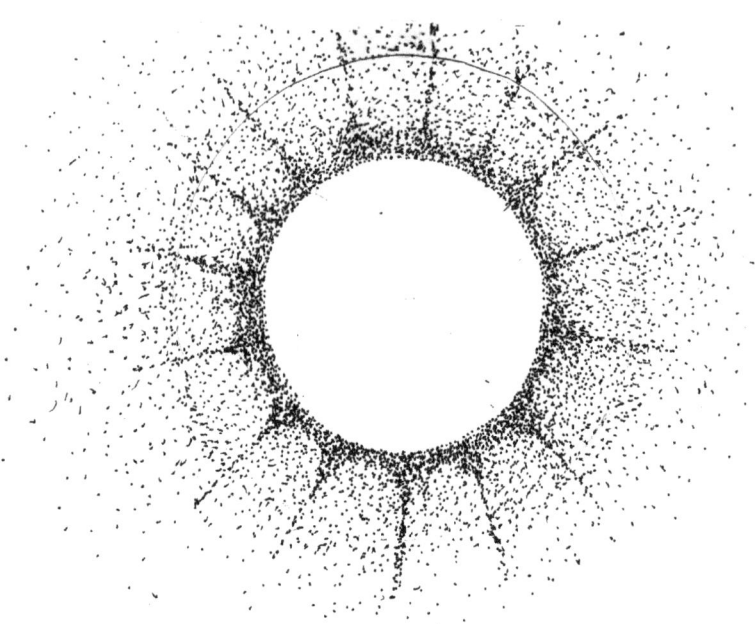

Just then, the clouds parted and the sun shone through. The sparkling sun danced over the ocean's crashing waves.

Harmony smiled. "I knew you were up there," she said.

Harmony kicked off her boots and ran barefoot through the sand. The sand flew into the air as she ran faster. She liked how the sand felt between her toes. And the way the sun warmed her shoulders. She felt the earth beneath her feet and the sun above her.

"I love the sun, Inti, and Mother Earth, Pachamama," Harmony said out loud.

Harmony giggled as she dashed down the beach toward home.

Harmony's Journal

 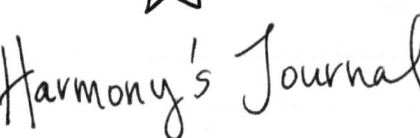  

Dear friend,

I am so excited you found this book! It means you are an explorer like me!

I hope you will add your own notes to this journal. It is something we can share. If you learn more about Inti Raymi or other things about Peru, you can add them to this journal AND to the **harmonymeetstheworld.com** website! Help others learn more about the world and other people. I think if we work together, we can make the world a better place. Let's each be our own best self and also a good friend to others.

With peace and love,
Harmony

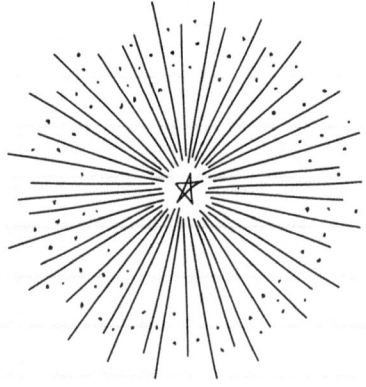

_____'s Journal
(write your name here)

Harmony's Question

During my adventure at Inti Raymi, I learned about the importance of the sun. What does the sun mean to you?
◎ Write or draw your answer below. ◎

Festival Facts

1. Inti Raymi is one of the biggest festivals in South America.

2. Cusco celebrates Inti Raymi every year on June 24th during the winter solstice, when the sun is the farthest from Peru. The festival honors the return of Father Sun.

3. The festival also marks the start of the Andean New Year. Coca leaves are read at the Plaza de Armas to reveal the fortune of the upcoming year.

4. After the Spanish soldiers banned Inti Raymi in the 1570s, the festival was brought back by Faustino Espinoza Navarro in the 1940s. He was both a scholar and actor. He played the role of the Sapa Inca for 12 years.

5. Although Inti Raymi is a re-creation today, it's still a religious ceremony as it was during ancient Inca times.

6. Hundreds of dancers and performers, dressed in vibrant hand-crafted costumes, bring the Inca culture alive.

7. The soft melodic voices of acllas can be heard during the festival. Acllas are chosen young women who sing to the sun god Inti and the Sapa Inca.

8. Tawantinsuyu was the name for the Inca Empire. It was divided into four parts or quadrants called suyus. People from these suyus are represented during the festival.

9. The Peruvian government proclaimed Inti Raymi as Peru's cultural heritage in 2001.

10. As the ceremony concludes at the ancient fortress of Sacsayhuaman, the performers parade back to the city of Cusco.

Peru Facts

1. Cusco was the ancient Inca capital. It was considered to be the belly button of the earth. Today, the capital of Peru is Lima.

2. Nestled high in the Andes mountains, Cusco has an altitude of 3,399 meters. Many people chew coca leaves to help prevent altitude sickness.

3. It's said that the city of Cusco is shaped like a puma.

4. Potatoes are one of the most grown vegetables in Peru. Thousands of different kinds of potatoes are harvested.

5. Peru is known for its hand-crafted textiles such as alpaca sweaters and Andean woolen caps called chullos. Don't forget to bring your soles—that's Peruvian money.

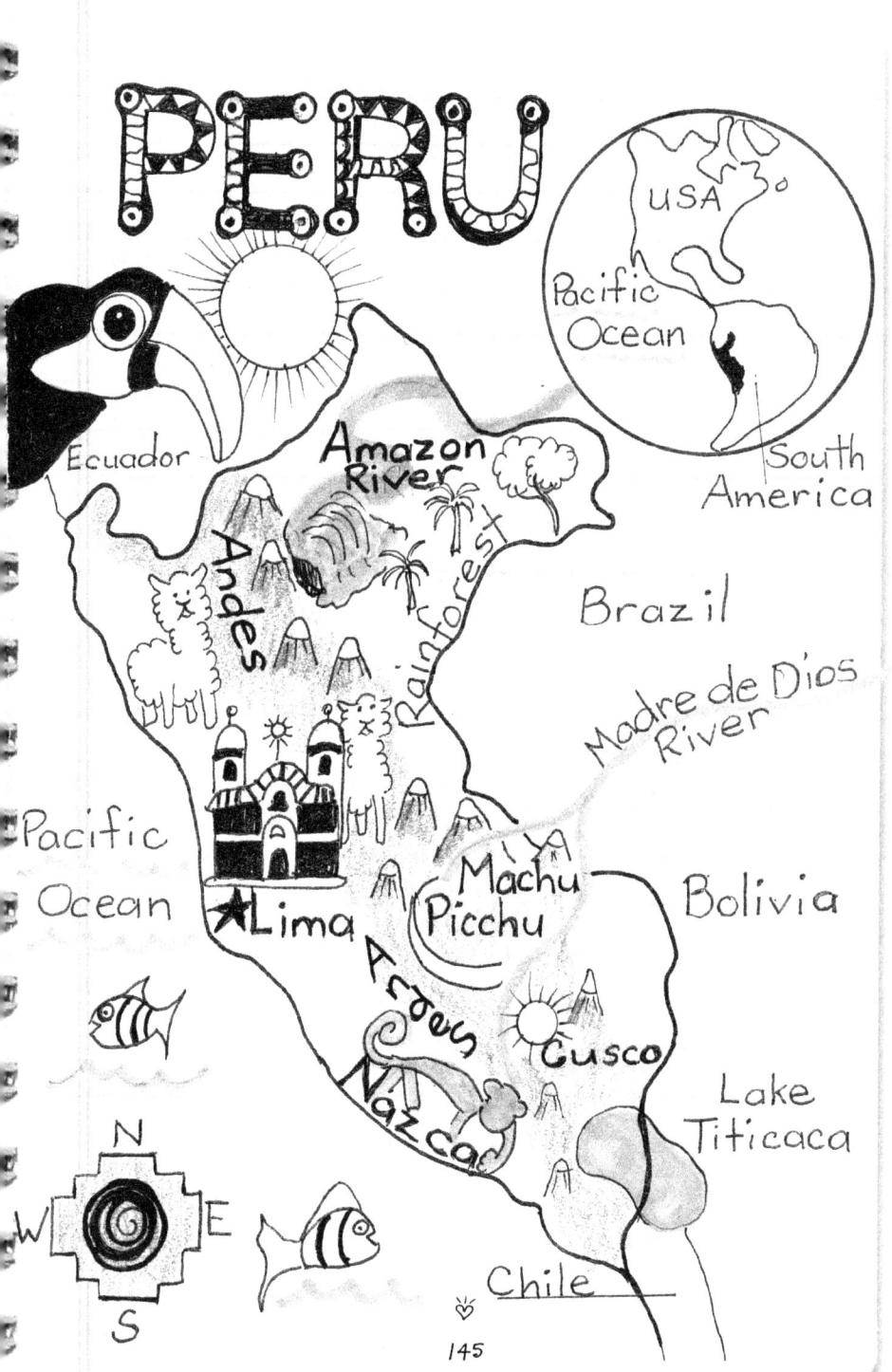

Inca Culture

What is the Inca Cross?

The Inca cross is a calendar. On it we see important festivals for each year. Every corner represents a month of the year. Each step is a model of Inca culture.

The first three steps represent three realms:
1. Condor brings messages to and from Heaven.
2. Puma represents Earth and courage.
3. Snake belongs to the Underworld. It is wisdom.

The following steps show us how to behave:
4. Help out your family with their work and they will help you.
5. Connect to the community. Share happiness.
6. Participate in community work.
7. Don't be selfish.
8. Don't be lazy.
9. Don't steal.
10. Love yourself—share love.
11. Love your work.
12. Love knowledge and learning.

Center: Cusco is the center of the Inca World. It has spiritual wisdom and power.

Source: Daniel Mayta Perez, Alpaca Expeditions, YouTube.com

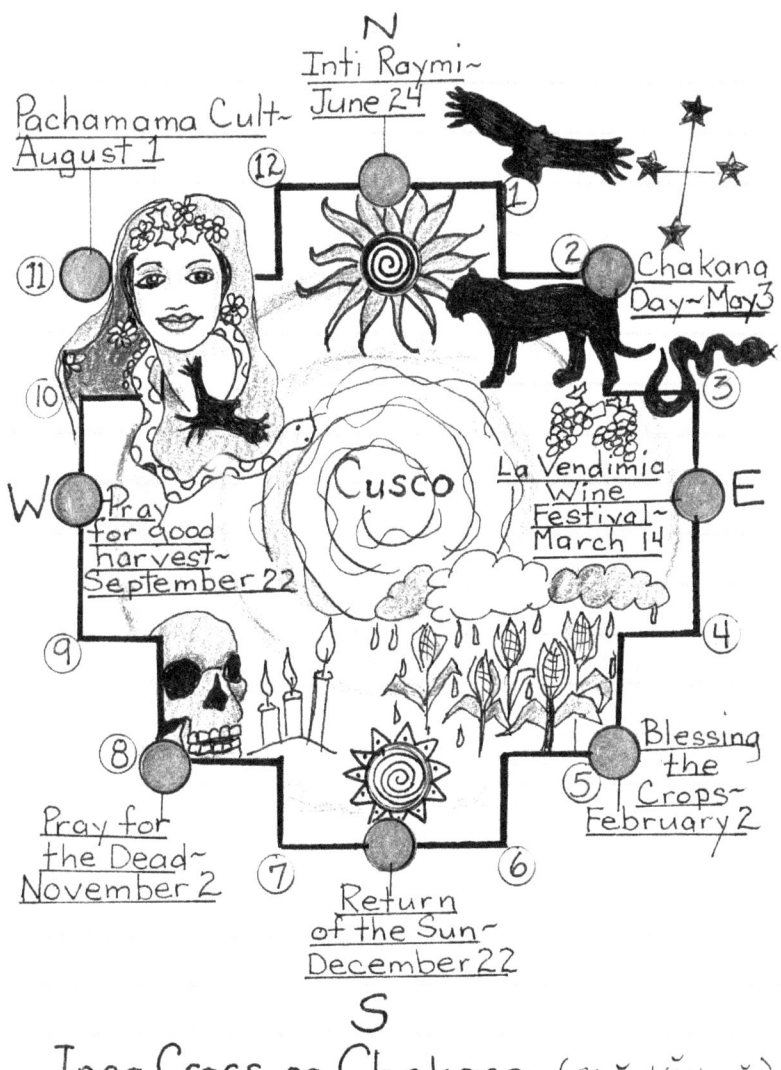

Inca Cross or Chakana (shă KĂH nă)

Learn the Language

Quechua (kech-wah) is an ancient Inca language. It's one of the main languages spoken in Peru today alongside Spanish and Aymara. Quechua is also spoken in other countries such as Bolivia, Argentina, Columbia, and Ecuador. There are many different dialects of the Quechua language depending on the region in which it's spoken. Approximately 8 million people speak Quechua.

Here's a fun project –

Cut and fold to make your own mini Quechua language book!

FOLD-A-BOOK
Instructions

Need a video tutorial? Find one at harmonymeetstheworld.com!

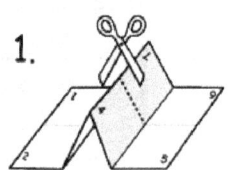

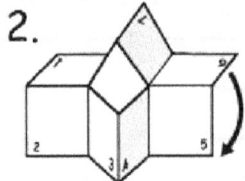

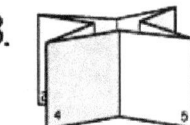

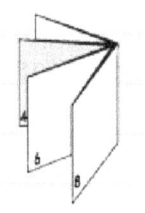

QUECHUA

Harmony Meets the World
LEARN THE LANGUAGE

Collection of:

_____
(write your name here)

TUPANANCHISCAMA

When it's time to say goodbye, try the phrase: Tupananchiscama. Even though the word looks hard to say, it's pronounced (two-pa-nahn-cheese-kama). It's akin to "see you next time."

MUNAKUYKI

It never hurts to spread some kindness. The Quechua language has many phrases to show affection. For instance, munakuyki means I love you. It's pronounced: (moon-ah-koo-ah-key). Go ahead and spread the love!

COUNT TO TEN

1 – huk (hook)
2 – iskay (ee-sky)
3 – kimsa (keem-sah)
4 – tawa (tah-wah)
5 – pichqa (peech-nah)
6 – suqta (sookh-tah)
7 – qanchis (kahn-cheese)
8 – pusaq (poo-sah)
9 – isqun (ees-koohn)
10 – chunka (choon-kah)

Listen to the pronunciations at:
http://andes.org/audio/count.wav

GREETINGS

Whether it's morning, noon, or night, it's always pleasant to receive a warm greeting. The word Napaykuna (pronounced Nah-pie-koon-nah) means greetings.

Here are some you can use:

Hello:
Allillanchu (Ah-lee-yahn-chu)

Good morning:
Allin Punchay (Ah-leen Poon-chay)

Good Afternoon:
Allin Suka (Ah-leen Sue-kah)

Good Evening:
Allin Tuta (Ah-leen Too-tah)

SULPAYKI

When someone lends a helping hand, gives you a compliment, or does something nice for you, you'll need this Quechua phrase: Sulpayki. It means thank you. It's pronounced: (sool-pay-ki). So next time you want to show your gratitude, give this phrase a try.

149

✂ Add your own notes to the inside of the language book! ✂

Glossary

** some words you might need help understanding **

Abalone (abba-loan-ee) shell: These shells are found on the beach, often on the coast of California and around the world. A mollusk or sea creature lives inside. You can spot these shells because the inside is colorful and has a shimmering quality.

Chinkanas (Chee-kahn-as): Secret tunnels. Chinkana comes from the Quechua word meaning labyrinth or underground tunnel. These tunnels are hidden under the city of Cusco. It's said the Inca hid their gold in these secret tunnels.

Coya (Coy-yah): The Inca queen.

Driftwood: A piece of wood often found on the beach or floating in the ocean.

Hermit Crab: A crab that lives in empty shells left by other sea creatures. When the crab grows bigger, he moves into a bigger shell. Hermit crabs love to climb and explore.

Huacatay (Wok-ah-tie): A Peruvian black mint. It's grown in the Andes mountains. This herb is used in chicken and fish dishes. Also, it's often used in teas to help cure colds and stomach aches.

Inca (Ink-ah): A large, powerful, ancient civilization in South America. The Inca Empire flourished between 1438-1532. It was an empire rich with gold and silver.

Inti (In-tee): The Inca sun god.

Inti Raymi (In-tee Rye-me): Translates as Sun Festival. It's an Inca religious ceremony dedicated to the Sun god Inti.

Pachacutec (Pach-ah-cu-tech): The ninth Sapa Inca, also known as Pachacuti. He expanded the Inca Empire and was responsible for helping build the historical site Machu Picchu. He also started Inti Raymi.

Pachamama (Pa-cha-mama): Mother Earth. A respected goddess of the Inca. She provides food, water, and shelter. She is the holder and preserver of life.

Plaza de Armas (Plaza de Arm-as): Cusco's main square.

Poncho (Pon-cho): A piece of clothing that falls over one's shoulders. It's loose-fitting and often made of alpaca wool. Ponchos are designed with a variety of colors and patterns. They keep one warm and protected from cold and rainy weather.

Pututu (Puh-too-too): An ancient instrument used in the Andean culture. It's made from a conch shell (sea snail shell). It has a mouthpiece similar to a trumpet. When blown into, it makes a commanding sound. This instrument is used to call special meetings, important events, and celebrate festivals.

Sacsayhuaman (Sahk-say-wah-mahn): An ancient fortress built of stone. It was used during the Inca Empire. It's located just outside the city of Cusco, Peru. Some of its largest stones are said to weigh over 120 tons.

Sapa Inca (Sah-pa Ink-ah): The emperor. He was the head of the Inca Empire and made the laws. The Inca believed he was the direct descendant of the Sun god, Inti.

Sun Temple: Also known as **Qorikancha (Kori-Kon-cha)** which means "Golden Temple" in Quechua. This sacred temple was built by the Inca. It was dedicated to their Sun god, Inti. During the Inca Empire, the temple was covered in gold. After the Spanish invasion, the Sun Temple was destroyed, stripped of its gold, and the Santo Domingo Catholic church was built on top. Today, only a portion of the Sun Temple can be seen in the city of Cusco.

Suyus (Sue-yous): The four parts or regions of the Inca Empire. They were: The **Antisuyu** (Amazon rainforest), **Chinchaysuyu** (farming region), **Contisuyu** (the sea), and **Collasuyu** (the High Plains).

Tide pools: These are found on the beach near the shore. They're made of rocky areas filled with pockets of ocean water. You can find sea creatures living there. Some include: sea urchins, hermit crabs, and sea stars.

My Glossary

A place to add words you learn –

A Taste of Peru

Chicha morada is a popular Peruvian drink. It's made with purple corn. I LOVED trying this new drink that Apichu introduced me to. If you can find some purple corn, ask a grown-up to help you. And don't forget to check if anyone has a food allergy.

Make this sweet drink on a hot afternoon!

Chicha Morada Sweet Drink Recipe*

Delicious purple corn superfood beverage from Peru
Prep Time: 20 minutes
Cook Time: 1 hour 30 minutes
Total Time: 1 hour 50 minutes
Servings: 10

Ingredients
- 2 pounds dried purple corn
- 1 ripe pineapple
- 3 medium quinces
- 2 apples sour
- 2 large peaches
- 8 whole cloves
- 2 cinnamon sticks
- 1 gallon (16 cups) of water
- 5 juice of limes
- 1 cup sugar

* Recipe courtesy of Keith at www.eatperu.com

-ॄ♡ॄ-

Directions

1. Wash the dried purple corn. Peel the pineapple, set aside the peel and heart. Peel and chop the apples and quinces.

2. Place the pineapple peel and heart, dried purple corn, apples, quinces, cinnamon sticks, and whole cloves into a large pot and add the water.

3. Boil for 90 minutes until the water turns to a dark purple color. Strain to remove the solid ingredients. Add sugar to taste and set aside to cool.

4. Add the lime juice when it has completely cooled.

5. Add tiny peach cubes before serving.

6. Serve with ice if you want an extra refreshing drink!

-ॄ♡ॄ-

Add your own notes here about what you liked (or what you changed) about the Chicha morada drink:

Resources

My friends helped me create a website with a bunch of really fun activities and more information about what I learned during my visit to Peru.

Check out the website when you can: www.harmonymeetstheworld.com

There are games, puzzles, videos, and free downloadable PDFs for teachers, parents, home-school educators, and librarians!

Resources include:

- Curriculum Guide
- Discussion Questions
- Math at the San Pedro Market
- Crossword Puzzle
- Sun-themed Activity

You can also order other books, special **Harmony meets the World** collectables, and learn about subscription boxes!

Also on the website you can learn about the club my friends and I created! **The Crystal Cove Club!** We look forward to meeting you and hearing your reaction to this series! Thank you for being a part of the adventure!
♡Harmony♡

About the Authors

Erin K. Schonauer and Jamie C. Schonauer are identical twins and write together as a team. They're award-winning authors of the nonfiction book *Early Burbank*. Their work has also appeared in children's magazines and has been internationally produced.

As twins, they share a close bond and a passion for storytelling. Their interest in writing and storytelling was sparked at an early age when they visited their local library and immersed themselves in the world of books. Here, they cherished some of their fondest memories like reading *The Baby-Sitters Club* and *Sweet Valley Twins*. The sisters have been writing together for over 10 years and especially have a tender spot for writing children's stories.

Erin and Jamie's unique bond as twins makes writing twice as fun! Plus, they are best friends!

Connect with the sisters at: www.twinpens.com

Erin (bottom) and Jamie (top)

Can you guess who's who?

About the Illustrator

I started out as a cowgirl in Chicago. Now, I am an artist in Arizona. How did that happen? Ever since I could remember I have loved art. I learned to paint and draw at the American Academy of Art in Chicago. After that, I went to college so I could become an art teacher. There I earned a Bachelor Degree in Art Education, and eventually earned a Master Degree in Art Education and another in the Humanities.

For over thirty years, it was a privilege for me to teach children and adults from kindergarten through college. I discovered that anyone can learn to be an artist. You only have to want to be one.

I am an author, artist, and poet. I work in many media including collage and jewelry design and anything that makes me happy. We all need to express what is inside of us – and to live a happy life.

Best Regards,
Kathleen

Read my blog at: jkschonauer.wordpress.com

CPSIA information can be obtained
at www.ICGtesting.com
Printed in the USA
JSHW052002081122
32853JS00006B/145